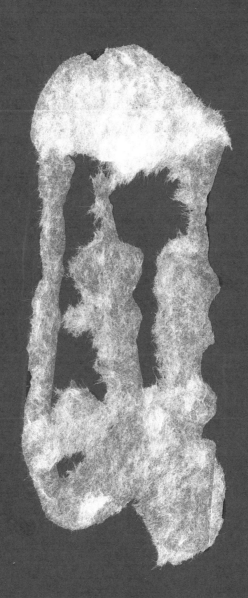

WAKE UP, FARM!

For India, Andy, and of course, Loren—A.T.

For Donna—C.E.

Inquiries should be addressed to Lothrop, Lee & Shepard Books, a division of
William Morrow & Company, Inc., 1350 Avenue of the Americas, New York, New York 10019.
Printed in the United States of America.
First Edition 1 2 3 4 5 6 7 8 9 10
Library of Congress Cataloging in Publication Data
Tresselt, Alvin R. Wake up, farm! / by Alvin Tresselt; illustrations by Carolyn Ewing.
p.   cm. Summary: Relates the morning activities and sounds of a variety of farm
animals.   ISBN 0-688-08654-3.—ISBN 0-688-08655-1 (lib. bdg.)   [1. Animal sounds—
Fiction.   2. Morning—Fiction.   3. Domestic animals—Fiction.   4. Farm life—Fiction.]
I. Ewing, C. S., ill.   II. Title. PZ7.T732Wakf   1990   [E]—dc20
90-33646 CIP AC

ALVIN TRESSELT

WAKE UP, FARM!

PICTURES BY CAROLYN EWING

LOTHROP, LEE & SHEPARD BOOKS   NEW YORK

All through the night, while the bright stars shone
in the velvet sky, everything slept—
birds in their nests and cows in the fields,
horses in barns and children in their beds—
till the stars grew dim and the moon sank in the west.

Now is the time for the sun to rise.
The sky grows bright, and first one, two, then all the birds
begin to sing their morning songs to welcome the new day.
Wake up, farm!

The big fat rooster hears them
and he hops up onto a fence post.
Cock-a-doodle-doo! he crows. Wake up, chickens!
Wake up, farm!

The hens hear the rooster
and *cluck, cluck, cluck,* they wake up.
They flutter down to the ground and scratch
for yesterday's leftover corn.

The mother horse wakes in her stall
and licks her colt behind the ears.
Wake up to a new day!

The ducks waddle out of the bushes by the brook.
They waggle their tails and jump in for a swim.
With a noisy *quack, quack, quack,* they say it's time to wake up!

Oink! Grunt! The roly-poly pigs root about in their pen, looking for their breakfast.

The gray goose pokes her long neck out of her nest
in the grass and looks around at the new day.
Honk, honk, honk! Wake up, farm!

The turkey wakes, too.
He flaps to the ground, spreads his feathers,
and parades about. How proud he looks.

The donkey hears all the noise
and opens his sleepy big brown eyes.
He wiggles his long, soft ears and snorts.
Even the sleepy donkey is waking.

Now the sheep and lambs come out of the sheepfold
to eat the dew-damp grass. With a soft *baaaa-h* the mothers
call their babies to stay near.

The strutting pigeons fly out of the dovecote
and circle about over the big red barn.
Coooo, coooo, coooo! Wake up, farm!

With a big stretch and a wide, wide yawn, tabby cat wakes up.
She purrs a rumbly *purrrr*
as she gives her kittens their morning bath.

Even the dog is wide awake. He barks at a chattering chipmunk who is looking for a leftover tidbit in the feeding dish. *Bow, wow, wow!* Everybody wake up!

Inside his hutch a warm, furry rabbit
twitches his wiggly nose and nibbles a carrot for breakfast.

Buzz-z-z-z-z-z! The buzzy, busy bees come out of their hives
and hover around the pink clover,
looking for sweet nectar to make honey.

The impatient cows are awake and waiting.
Moo, moo, moo! Time for milking!
Time for a meal of good grain. Wake up, farm!

And here comes the farmer, already tending his animals,
just as the sun comes over the hill.

At last a little boy in the big farmhouse opens his eyes.
He hears the birds singing and the animals calling.
The bright morning sun is shining in his window.
Now the whole farm is awake.
"Breakfast!" calls his mother. "Come and get it!"

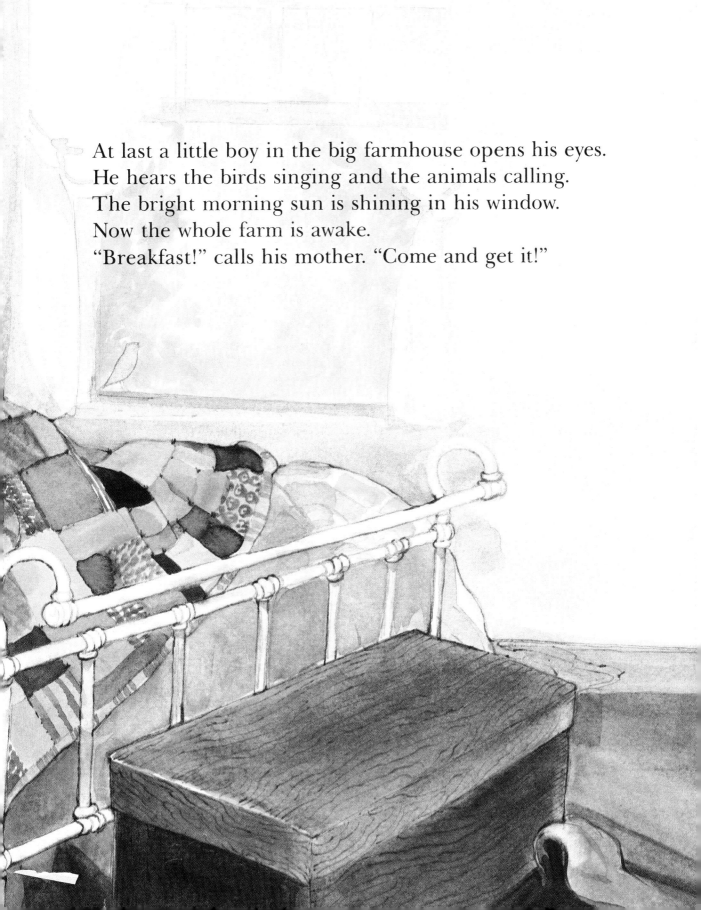

Another day has begun. Good morning, farm!

Alvin Tresselt writes for very young children in a very special way. Using the simplest, clearest language, he introduces readers to the basic facts and moods of the world around them. Noted for the poetic quality of his prose, Tresselt's books have awakened thousands of readers and listeners to the many small miracles of life. *Rain Drop Splash*, with illustrations by Leonard Weisgard, was a Caldecott Honor Book in 1946, and *White Snow, Bright Snow,* illustrated by Roger Duvoisin, was the winner of the 1947 Caldecott Medal.

Wake Up, Farm! was first published in 1955 with illustrations by Roger Duvoisin. Mr. Tresselt has updated the text of this new edition, enhancing its appeal to a new generation of readers. New full-color paintings by Carolyn Ewing provide a fresh contemporary setting.

Mr. Tresselt lives in Redding, Connecticut. Ms. Ewing lives in Kansas City, Missouri.